A DAY WITH A CONSTRUCTION WORKER

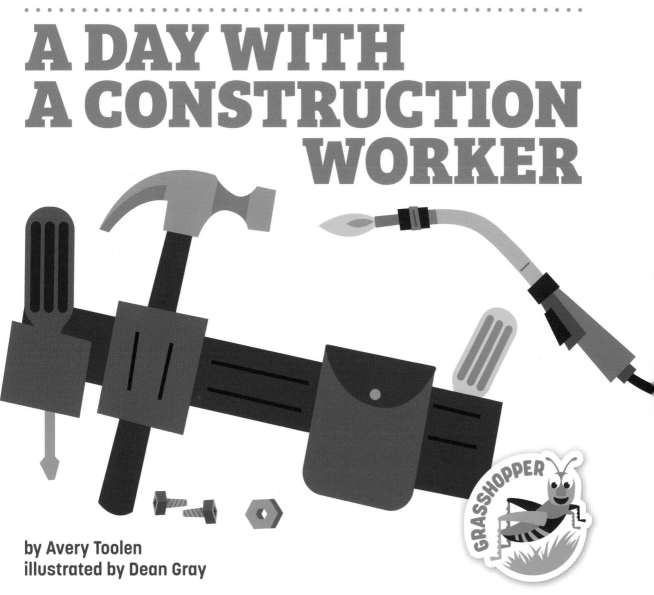

by Avery Toolen
illustrated by Dean Gray

Tools for Parents & Teachers

Grasshopper Books enhance imagination and introduce the earliest readers to fiction with fun storylines and illustrations. The easy-to-read text supports early reading experiences with repetitive sentence patterns and sight words.

Before Reading

- Discuss the cover illustration. What do they see?

- Look at the picture glossary together. Discuss the words.

Read the Book

- Read the book to the child, or have him or her read independently.

- "Walk" through the book and look at the illustrations. Who are the main characters? What is happening in the story?

After Reading

- Prompt the child to think more. Ask: Would you like to be a construction worker? Why or why not?

Grasshopper Books are published by Jump!
5357 Penn Avenue South
Minneapolis, MN 55419
www.jumplibrary.com

Library of Congress Cataloging-in-Publication Data

Names: Toolen, Avery, author. | Gray, Dean, illustrator.
Title: A day with a construction worker / by Avery Toolen; illustrated by Dean Gray.
Description: Minneapolis, MN: Jump!, Inc., 2022.
Series: Meet the community helpers!
Includes index.
Audience: Ages 5-8.
Identifiers: LCCN 2021034314 (print)
LCCN 2021034315 (ebook)
ISBN 9781636903255 (hardcover)
ISBN 9781636903262 (paperback)
ISBN 9781636903279 (ebook)
Subjects: LCSH: Readers (Primary)
Construction workers–Juvenile fiction.
LCGFT: Readers (Publications)
Classification: LCC PE1119.2 .T6633 2022 (print)
LCC PE1119.2 (ebook)
DDC 428.6/2–dc23
LC record available at https://lccn.loc.gov/2021034314
LC ebook record available at https://lccn.loc.gov/2021034315

Editor: Eliza Leahy
Direction and Layout: Anna Peterson
Illustrator: Dean Gray

Printed in the United States of America at Corporate Graphics in North Mankato, Minnesota.

Table of Contents

Building a Home 4

Quiz Time! 22

Construction Workers' Tools 22

Picture Glossary 23

Index 24

To Learn More 24

It is early. Construction workers start their day. They are building a house!

They wear vests, hard hats, and work boots.

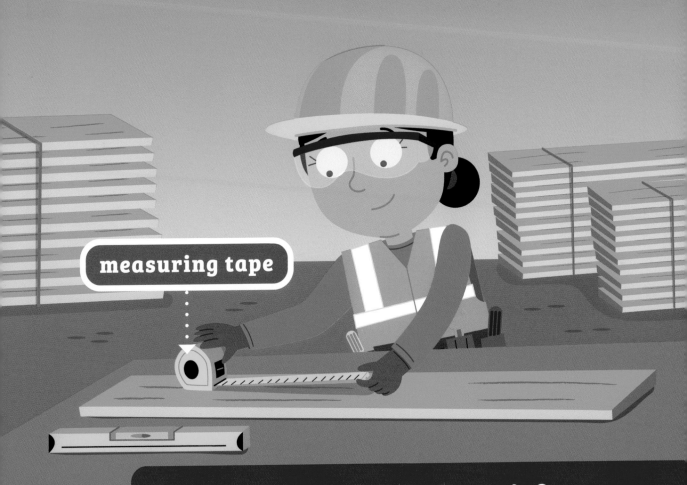

measuring tape

The workers build the house's frame.

Luisa measures the wood.

She uses a measuring tape.

Dax cuts the wood with a saw.

He wears safety glasses.

safety glasses

saw

Workers nail the pieces together.

Together, they lift the walls.

They weld the frame to beams.

This keeps the frame strong.

beam

frame

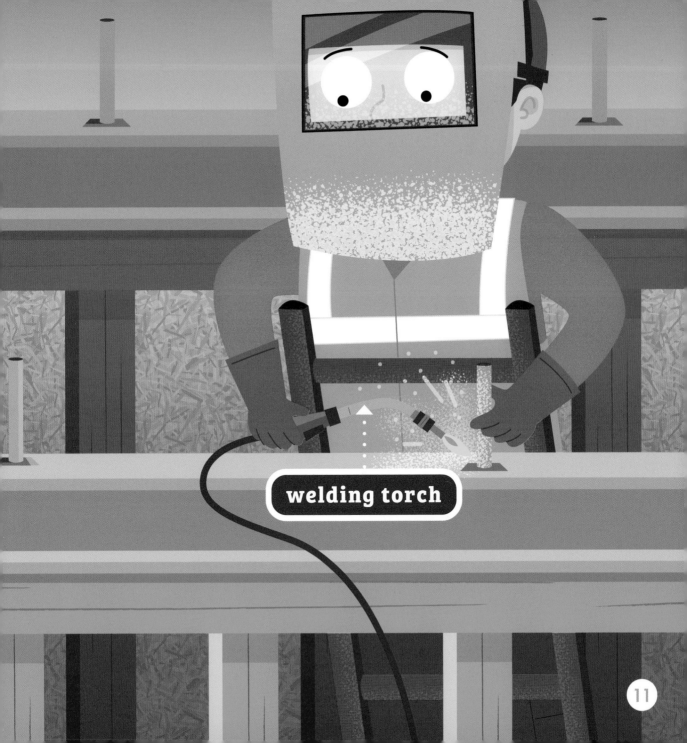

welding torch

Next, workers put in windows.

They put in doors, too.

window

Carla drives a bulldozer.

She clears an area.

The garage will go here!

Ricky drives a forklift.

It carries bricks.

bricks

Others start placing the bricks.

They make a wall.

17

Next, they start the roof.

Workers are careful.

They hammer big
beams into place.

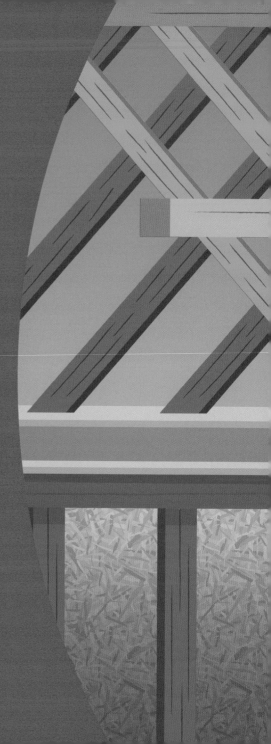

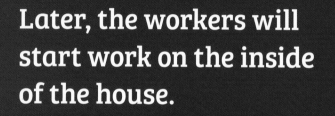

Later, the workers will start work on the inside of the house.

It has been a long morning.

For now, they take a break!

21

Quiz Time!

What does a forklift do?

       A. carries heavy items   **B.** clears debris
       C. saws wood   **D.** welds metal

Construction Workers' Tools

What tools do construction workers use? Take a look!

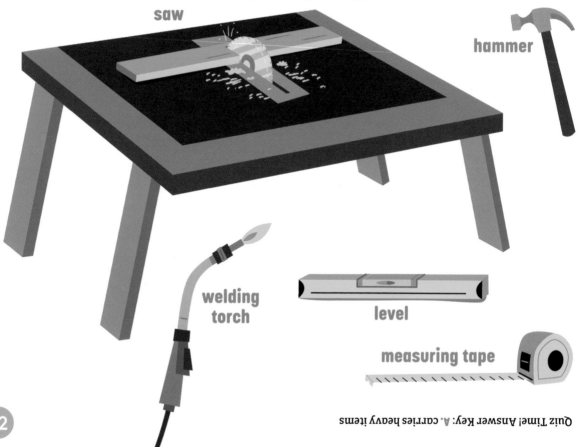

saw

hammer

welding torch

level

measuring tape

Picture Glossary

beams
Long, thick pieces of wood, concrete, or metal used as supports in buildings.

bulldozer
A powerful tractor with a broad, curved blade in front, used for clearing ground.

forklift
A vehicle with two long horizontal bars at the front, used for lifting and carrying heavy loads.

frame
A basic structure that provides support for a building.

safety glasses
Toughened glasses that protect the eyes when using power tools.

weld
To join two pieces of metal or plastic by heating them.

Index

beams 10, 18

bricks 16, 17

bulldozer 14

cuts 6

doors 12

forklift 16

frame 5, 10

garage 14

hammer 18

hard hats 4

measuring tape 5

nail 8

roof 18

saw 6

walls 9, 17

weld 10

windows 12

wood 5, 6

To Learn More

FACT SURFER

Finding more information is as easy as 1, 2, 3.

❶ Go to www.factsurfer.com

❷ Enter "**adaywithaconstructionworker**" into the search box.

❸ Choose your book to see a list of websites.